The shaman or sorceror-priest of the tribes living in the northern and Arctic latitudes of

Finland, Siberia and America is frequently classed as a psychopath. In spirit he flies up to

heaven, descends to hell and dives to the nethermost regions of the sea. He receives

messages from the dead, communes with spirits. But his mental balance is insecure and he is

easily 'unhinged'. If suddenly angered or startled he loses his self control completely.

His eyes redden and bulge out, his face goes through the most hideous contortions,

and unless restrained he will not hesitate to maim or murder the person who provoked him."

— from MAN, MYTH & MAGIC
by RICHARD CAVENDISH

"Gods and beasts, that is what our world is made of."

— Adolf Hitler, quoted in THE VOICE OF DESTRUCTION
by HERMAN RAUSCHNING

"The fog is rising..."

— EMILY DICKINSON, 1830-1886
(Last words.)

written by ALAN MOORE • drawn by EDDIE CAMPBELL

art assistance by PETE MULLINS & APRIL POST • logo by TODD KLEIN
chapter heading calligraphy by DES RODEN • cover by EDDIE CAMPBELL & APRIL POST
design and production by MICHAEL EASTMAN & TAMARA SIBERT

Chapter
Eight

Love
is
Enough

Miller's Court, September 22nd 1888.

Mrm It's a lovely arse you've got on ye, Marie Kelly.

And it's a dirty mouth ye've got on you, Joe Barnett. Go back to sleep!

I can't. I'm off down Billingsgate, lookin' for work. God, your hair's a lovely red where the sun catches.

Ha! It's drinking money you're after, is it?

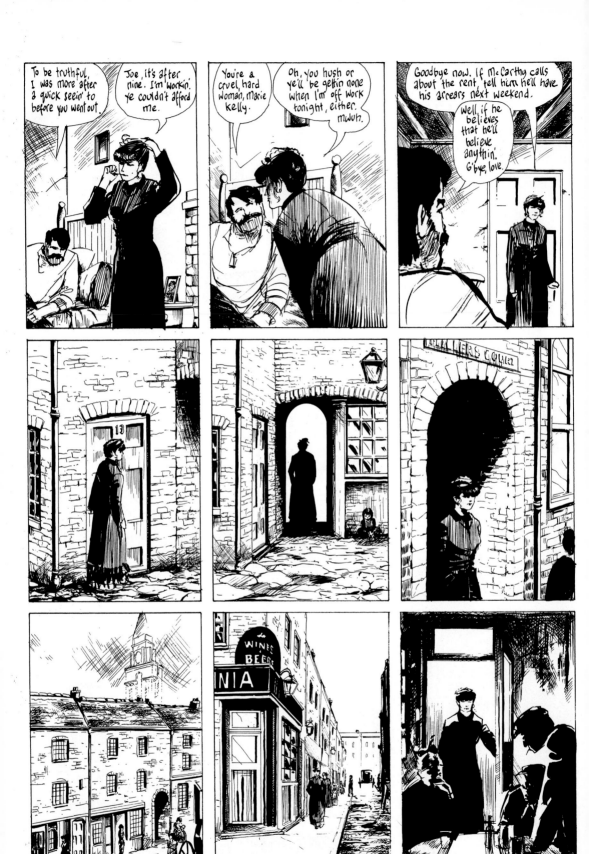

From Hell Chapter 8 page 2.

God, Kate Eddowes, but you're a marvel. How old is it y'are now? Your sister said you was forty-three...

Ha! that's what she knows!

Anyway. fancy askin' a woman's age when you've just 'ad 'er. Not that I could tell you. Can't remember. Old enough.

An' what's this on your arm? this "T.C."?

You KNOW what it is! I 'ad it done in Wolverhampton when I left 'ome with old Tommy Conway. I were just nineteen.

Good ride was he?

Oh, you've no competition. Though he didn't do bad, for a pensioner. Lived off these chapbooks 'e wrote. We 'ad three kids.

Not that the little buggers 'ave lifted a finger for me since I left the blind drunk old brute. My Annie, she avoids me now she's married.

Oh, never you mind her, snotty little madam she is. I was thinkin' we might go hop-pickin', you and me. Over in Kent. M?

From Hell Chapter 8 page 6.

Haloo! I Say, Eddie!

Whatevers the matter, old chap? No sooner do we get here to Abergeldie than you're off mooning about on the moors!

Dear Jem. I was thinking about London. All the terrible things that happen. These murders...

Eddie, Do buck up! You came to Scotland to get away from London for a bit.

Whitechapel's MILES away, Eddie. Anyway, what's two whores less?

Jem... those women. They didn't deserve to die. Not like that. They hadn't DONE anything

Oh, Eddie! Come OFF it! They were WOMEN! They must have done SOMETHING.

It isn't funny. Jem.

Eddie, I was JOKING, Alright? I just can't see why you're so concerned about wretched hags that you don't even know.

From Hell Chapter 8 page 8.

...unless you want to count Polly Nichols. 'Er who got done in.

Look, if you see her tell her to contact WALTER. She's in danger. Terrible danger.

Two hundred pounds

John? Kelly!

John, let's drop all this and go back to London TONIGHT. I've an idea that can make us some money.

Oh aye? I know about your ideas for earnin' money! Still, you're right about these hops. They're shite

I've just got a FEELING, John.

Well, you're feelin alright t'me.

Stop it. No, it's just I feel I have to be in London tomorrow. It's IMPORTANT say we can go, John?

Aah, Katey Eddowes! How can I say no when you're gazin' like that? London it is, me love. We'll see what fortune's got in store for ye.

Hello, Fred.

Oh, Emma. It's you. I was 'opin' I might run into you. I'm just 'ere on me dinner break, like. Can I get you a drink

No, it's kind of ye, but I mustn't stop. I'm only passin' through. There's money needs earnin'. Badly.

Why, what's up? You're not y' know, in trouble?

No! No, not like THAT! It...it's just this DEBT I have.

God, Fred, if I don't find some money somewhere, I don't know WHAT'll become of me.

If only I'd decent work, like you with your SADDLE-MAKIN'. Oh, Fred, I'm sorry to burden ye.

Perhaps I could find the money. I don't know, but...

Oh, Fred, I couldn't...

Don't be daft! Look, if it'll get you out of an 'ole, I'd be glad to! I dunno what I've got on me...

Look, there's two quid. I know it's not much, but...

Well, I know you've spent time nattering with me when you could be out earnin' money, so...

Fred, I...I don't know what to say. I can take this and pay off me debt. You've saved me life.

Huh! S'what friends are for, ennit?

Aye. And ye never want t'bed me for the privilege. You're a good friend, Fred.

A real friend

CORONERS REPORT

DATE 26th Sept. 1888

CORONER Wynne Baxter

Summing up at inquest of
Eliza Anne Chapman

appears that
wounds inflic
caused, exten
as well as
the long...

The injuries were made by someone with considerable anatomical skill. They were no meaningless cuts. The conclusion that the desire was to possess the missing abdominal organ seems overwhelming.

Recently, an American visited London medical institutions offering £20 for specimens of the uterus. He intended to issue one with each copy of a publication he was preparing.

I suggest that the American's request, though refused, might have incited some abandoned wretch to possess himself of a specimen. That, Gentlemen, is my considered opinion.

By trade a butcher, Joseph Issenschmidt suffered a mental breakdown when his business failed. During 1887 he spent ten weeks in Colney Hatch Asylum.

On September 8th, following Chapman's murder, Mrs Fiddymount, landlady of the Prince Albert in Brushfield Street saw a bloodstained man, possibly Issenschmidt drinking in her bar

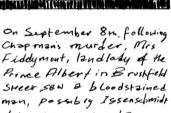

On September 17th, questioned by Sergeant Thick at Fairfield Road Asylum, Bow. Issenschmidt revealed he had told numerous woman in Holloway that he was "Leather Apron"

He collected sheep's heads feet and kidneys from the market for sale in the West End, explaining his absences and the blood.

He had left his wife after an argument"

Piggott arrived in Gravesend at 4.00 p.m. on Sunday September 9th, saying he'd walked from Whitechapel. At "The Pope's Head" he expressed hostility to women. The landlady called the police.

Sent to investigate, Superintendent Barry noticed a bite on Piggott's hand, allegedly received from a woman in a backyard behind a Whitechapel lodging house.

There were blood spots upon a shirt in his bag and the Police surgeon was of the opinion that his shoes had recently been wiped clean of blood.

Inspector Abberline took him to Whitechapel for an identity parade before Mrs. Fiddymont and others, who failed to identify him. He was sent to Whitechapel Workhouse Infirmary.

From Hell Chapter 8 page 16.

Oy! Oy, 'ang on! What's all this 'n aid of?

Oh, Frederick, I do love you so very much.

Last night you were talking in your sleep, you know. You said the sweetest thing.

Oh, for God's sake, what are you on about now, woman?

You said "Emma". "Oh, Emma".

From Hell Chapter 8 page 18.

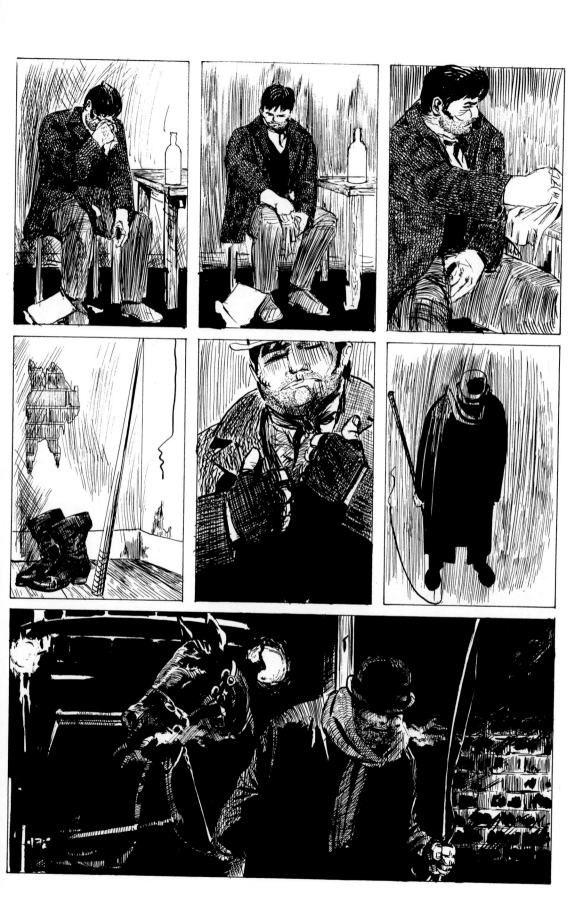

From Hell Chapter 8 page 19.

B· beggin' yer pardon, Sir William, but shall we be, y' know...

Tonight, shall we be, like, doin' one?

A woman.

Hmm? No, no... not tonight. Tonight you must take me to the Mitre Tavern, in Mitre Square.

There's a policeman there, you see.

He wants a word with me.

Then join hand in hand...

T'each other firm stand...

Oh my God.

The next woman will be taken tomorrow night. "Mary Jane Kelly" meanwhile proves elusive.

Let's be merry and put a bright face on...

If any brothers in your employ LOCATE her, I MUST be informed IMMEDIATELY.

Gull please, in the name of reason...

What mortal can boast...

Invoke not Reason. In the end it is too small a deity.

Good Evening to you, sir.

So noble a toast...

As a free and accepted mason...

ALES

Home.

..say you found 'er Lou?

Aldgate High Street, fast asleep. Come on, let's get 'er inside and booked. Up a bit your side, George.

Make room, Sarge. Found 'er in Aldgate High Street. She's pissed.

Blimey, you DO surprise me, Robinson.

C'mon, darlin', What's your name?

Nothin...

Huh. Nothing's about right for the likes of you. Ah well, get 'er down 'the cells, lads. No identification on 'er was there?

No, No. I didn't see any. She's dragging your side, George..

'Ere, what about that PAWN TICKET in 'er mustard tin? THAT 'ad a name on it!

oh, that's right. There was a pawn ticket, Sarge. In a tin she was carryin'. Name on it was Jane Kelly.

George, for fuck's sake, she's slipping...

Whoah! There. A quarter to twelve. One hour on the dot, like I said. Glad to see you waited for me.

'is Lordship's inside. This is 'er, Sir William, the one I gave the flower to.

Ah! Ah yes. You are Elizabeth, I think. Tell me, Elizabeth, do you like grapes?

I..yes, sir. Very much I like grapes.

Then have some.

Perhaps there is somewhere nearby that we might go? My coachman will keep watch, yes?

Aye, sir.

This way. There is a place.

HINDLEY SACK MAKER

Oh, yes. This will do splendidly, I...

Child? Whatever is the matter?

It...ughh...it is these grapes. They have something on them, I think.

'tis laudanum. A little, nothing more.

They are the grapes of mercy, child, not lightly spat away.

If I could have your attention, gentlemen...

I'm returned from walking my lady home, but before those left after tonight's discussion begin more Russian songs, a regular guest has a POEM...

our comrade Mr. William Morris

Thank you, brothers. Next week I'll be reciting my "Chants for Socialists," but tonight an older work might suffice." It's entitled "Love is Enough".

"Love is Enough: Have no thought for tomorrow, / if ye lie down this even in rest from your pain."

"ye who have paid for our bliss with great sorrow, / for as it was once so shall it be again.

"ye shall cry out for death as you stretch forth in vain"...

From Hell- chapter 8 - page 31.

Let's not do any more, Sir, ay? Not on this one, ay? I keep thinkin' I 'ear somebody comin'.

Yes... Yes, I remember now...

This is the one that I didn't finish, isn't it?

S- Sir William Gull?

Has this... Has this happened before?

I ... I went to Brook Street. Your wife, Lady Gull, she said you had a patient in Whitechapel. Described your coach.

Hours, sir, I've been looking.

I- It's the woman, sir. Kelly. We've got her at Bishopgate lock-up. But they throw out the drunks at one. You'll have to hurry.

From Hell - Chapter 8, page 33.

"Mary Kelly". It's 'er, sir, an' I've got 'er description off the coppers. Left ten minutes back, headin' down Mitre Square way.

Mitre Square.

Alas, Sir Charles, the blood has reached your doorstep! Ha ha ha!

Drive on, Netley. Drive on.

Evenin' to ye, miss. Wet old night.

'ow d'ye fancy being somewhere dry 'an 'earnin' a few coppers into the bargain?

Oh, Aye? And where would that be?

In me coach, customer o' mine, old gent, needin' some company. It's just down here.

From Hell Chapter 8 page 37.

From Hell - Chapter 8 - Page 40.

Stop here. It doesn't matter if there is no trough; the worst of it is off.

I merely need somewhere to drop this bloodied rag.

How about that doorway, sir, just over there & it's dark enough...

No, Netley, you misunderstand. I WANT it to be found.

Although, upon consideration... tell me, Netley; do you have a piece of chalk about your person?

Chalk? Well, I usually keeps a bit about me, like, but why...?

Just give it to me, Netley. I've resolved to leave a MESSAGE.

Message, sir? Who to?

To one who'll know its MEANING. These four women were all TRAITORS, Netley, well deserving of their fate...

Just as the JUWES who slew Hiram Abiff were deserving of THEIR punishment... throats slit from left to right, entrails about their shoulders. Now, how to begin?

Why, the murders, woman. What else? When I heard about that Long Liz gettin' done in I was worried you'd been with her!

Liz?

Oh God, I'm sorry, love. I thought ye'd have heard already. Everybody's been talkin' about it.

Liz. What... what happened?

Cut up, like the others. Down Berner Street.

That weren't the worst of it, though. Done another one tonight, 'e 'ad.

A-another one?

Woman named Cathy Eddowes, down Mitre Square.

What scared ME, she'd given a FALSE NAME to the police earlier, and that's the name I heard first.

They said Mary Kelly had been cut to pieces.

A P P E N D I X

APPENDIX TO VOLUME FIVE:
CHAPTER EIGHT

PAGE 1-3

Little of novelty is established on these pages, save that Joseph Barnett, Marie Kelly's live-in lover, sometimes sought or found employment at Billingsgate fish market. The information that Barnett was a riverside laborer and market porter who was licensed to work at Billingsgate comes from *The Jack the Ripper A-Z* by Begg, Fido and Skinner (Headline Books, 1991). The fact that Marie Kelly was in arrears on her rent, suggested in panel three of page two, is supported by the same source, which gives Kelly's weekly rent as four shillings and sixpence, and relates that she was in arrears to the sum of thirty shillings at the time of her death in early November.

PAGES 4 & 5

The details of Catherine Eddowes' early life, and the decision made by her and her lover John Kelly to travel to Kent and earn money picking hops is as recounted in both *The JTR A-Z* and *JTR, The Uncensored Facts* by Paul Begg (Robson Books, 1988), amongst other sources.

PAGES 6 & 7

Although invented, this scene is a reconstruction of the alleged quarrel that led to Elizabeth Stride quitting her lodgings with Michael Kidney in Dorset Street and relocating in Flower & Dean Street during the September of 1888. According to Paul Begg in *JTR, The Uncensored Facts*, a woman named Catherine Lane reported that Stride had told her that she had left Kidney after a row, although the unfortunately-named Kidney denied this at the inquest. The details of Stride and Kidney's previous relationship are according to both *The JTR A-Z* and a welcome new addition to Ripper literature entitled *Jack the Myth* by A.P. Wolf (Robert Hale, 1993).

PAGE 8 & 9

The scene on these pages, while invented, is compiled from various known facts concerning the protagonists, Prince Albert Victor Christian Edward and his close friend J.K. "Jem" Stephen. That Prince Eddy was visiting Queen Victoria in Abergeldie, Scotland between the 27th and 30th of September is sustained by the Court Circulars, diaries, journals and letters of the period, as presented in

The JTR A-Z by Begg, Fido and Skinner. Although there is no evidence to suggest that Jem Stephen had accompanied Prince Eddy on this visit, his presence is at least made theoretically possible by the dates of his Cambridge vacations, as given in *Murder & Madness, The Secret Life of Jack the Ripper* by Dr. David Abrahamsen (Robson Books, 1992). If I may, I should like to take this opportunity to opine that Dr. Abrahamsen's book is one of the very worst pieces of Ripper literature that it has ever been my misfortune to read, based largely upon flights of theoretical psychoanalytic fancy that strain credulity at best and at worst are simply unsupportable. The most alarming thing about this tome is the fact that the author is apparently a forensic scientist and "expert witness" whose testimony might considerably decide whether somebody goes to prison or not. Read it and weep.

To return to the scene in hand, the portrayal of Stephen's character herein is based upon what can be construed of the man through his life and works. Genial and outgoing, he was also a rabid misogynist who expressed his feeling about the opposite sex in memorable stanzas such as the following, which concludes a description of a woman encountered while strolling "In the Backs," the college gardens bordering the River Cam. After complaining that the woman is "devoid of taste or shape or character," "dull," and "unthinking," he states that:

> "I should not mind
> If she were done away with, killed or ploughed,
> She did not seem to serve a useful end:
> And certainly she was not beautiful."

His relationship with Prince Eddy as depicted here, while speculative, is based upon suggestions made by others. Stephen was the Prince's tutor while at Cambridge, and his overt homosexuality coupled with the later connection between the Prince and the male brothel in Cleveland Street has led to strong suggestions that the two were lovers, as indicated by panel five on page nine. See *Clarence: The Life of the Duke of Clarence and Avondale KG, 1864-1892*, by Michael Harrison (W.H. Allen, 1972).

PAGE 10 & 11

The idea expressed on these pages, that Catherine Eddowes may have cut short her hop-picking jaunt in Kent because of a suspicion that she might be able to claim the reward by helping the police with their Whitechapel inquiries, is based upon Eddowes' subsequent remarks to her lodging-house Superintendent, just prior to her death: "I have come back to earn the reward offered for the apprehension of the Whitechapel murderer. I think I know him." Referring to this in *JTR, The Uncensored Facts*, Paul Begg very sensibly suggests that for want of any other evidence that Eddowes had information concerning the killings, it is perhaps best to treat the above statement as either a joke upon the part of Eddowes herself or an embellishment added by the lodging house Superintendent or the Press. Even so, Begg himself confesses that there is some room for doubt here, so I've decided to work the scene into the story as a fateful mistake on Cathy's part, based upon her chance meeting with Walter Sickert in Chapter Seven.

PAGE 12 - 17

While the opening scenes on pages 12 & 13, along with the scene on page 17, are inventions for story purposes that need no special explanation, more detailed treatment is required for the case notes that Abberline is seen reviewing on pages 14-16. The first of these, being a summary of coroner Wynne Baxter's summing up at the inquest of Annie Chapman, is quoted or reconstructed from the account given by Paul Begg in *JTR, The Uncensored Facts*, as are the case histories of Joseph Issenschmidt and William Piggott that follow it. The cases are included here as representative of the various suspects that were fruitlessly hauled in by the Police during this period, and they are by no means an exhaustive list.

PAGES 18 - 22

The scene here, with Sir Charles finally realizing the identity of the Royal personage directing Sir William, is an invention, although as usual it is constructed from real or quasi-real elements. The letter from Queen Victoria that Sir Charles refers to is genuine, and is made much of by Stephen Knight in *JTR: The Final Solution*. On the other hand, in *The JTR A-Z*, Fido, Begg, and Skinner suggest that by talking about "murders" in the plural at the time of the killing of Polly Nicholls, the Queen was simply following the then-popular misconception that Emma Elizabeth Smith had also been a victim of the Whitechapel murderer. You pays your money and you takes your choice.

The Mitre public house in Mitre Square is named as a Masonic meeting place in Knight's *JTR: The Final Solution*, and I have no reason to doubt him. The mitre, as a symbol, has strong Masonic ties, and I was unsurprised to learn

recently while addressing an occult forum of Chaos magicians, Wiccans and assorted Diabolists in a public house named The Mitre (right next to Hawksmoor's church St. Alfeges, in Greenwich) that the room was normally used by the local Freemasons.

The song being sung in the background during this scene is genuine, and is quoted from the entry on Freemasonry in *Man, Myth and Magic* by Richard Cavendish, a part-work published weekly by Purnell in the 1960s. I'm afraid that unless you also have access to the bound volumes, you're just going to have to trust me on this one.

PAGES 23 & 24

The fragmented sequence on these pages is an alcohol-fogged and time-lapsed contraction of the key events relating to Cathy Eddowes' return from Kent to London, parting with John Kelly and subsequently being arrested for drunkenness while in possession of a pawn ticket that gave her name as "Jane Kelly." The details are as related in most of the Ripper literature, including *The JTR A-Z* and Begg's *JTR, The Uncensored Facts*. The idea that a Masonic police officer may have been sent to find Dr. Gull after learning that the name of the detainee was similar to "Mary Jane Kelly" is an invention of my own, albeit one that is strongly implied in Knight's *JTR: The Final Solution*.

PAGE 25 & 26

The scene here, with Marie Kelly confronting the old Nichol mob and learning for the first time that they are not involved in the murder of her friends, is a fabrication for story purposes.

PAGE 27 - 33

The customer that Liz is seen with on page 27 is as described by witnesses J. Best and John Gardner, who saw her leave the Bricklayer's Arms with a man around eleven o'clock. The dialogue of Best and Gardner in this scene is more or less as related by the men themselves, quoted in *The JTR A-Z*. Dutfield's Yard, the destination to which Liz takes her customer, is as described by Paul Begg in *JTR, The Uncensored Facts*. Begg also notes the existence of the premises belonging to sack manufacturer Walter Hindley which looked out onto the yard, as glimpsed in panel five. The yard was often used by prostitutes plying their trade, making it a logical spot for Liz to entertain her clients. The scene with Netley and Liz Stride buying grapes on page 28 is according to the evidence of fruiterer Matthew Packer, who, as detailed in *The JTR A-Z*, reported that a man and a woman he later identified as Stride purchased a bag of grapes from him at some time between eleven and eleven forty-five on the evening in question. The remark made by Netley in panel two of page 29 is as reported by witness William Marshall (depicted in the foreground here) who, according to *The JTR A-Z*, was standing at the door of his lodgings at about 11:45 when he saw the man and woman standing across from him and heard the attributed remark. Roughly three-quarters of an hour later, P.G. William Smith saw a woman he later identified as Stride, walking along with a youngish man wearing a black diagonal coat and a hard felt hat. At this point, Stride was wearing a red flower on her coat. This information is from *JTR, The Uncensored Facts* by Paul Begg.

In the last two panels of page thirty we see Liz Stride spitting out the laudanum-painted grapes that Gull has offered her. This relates to evidence given by Dr. Bagster Phillips, among others, as related in *The JTR A-Z*. Dr. Phillips reported that Stride had definitely not eaten grape seeds or skins prior to her death, since these were not found in her stomach. He did, however, report that some stains on Stride's handkerchief were fruit juice, suggesting that the grapes may have been spat out. Detective Constable Walter Dew, according to the same source, also reported that spat-out grape seeds and skins had been found in the yard after a search by detectives. There is also the mystery of a grape stem allegedly found in the yard, which was at first reported in the newspapers and then seems to vanish from the evidence as if it had never been there, the implication being that the stem may have been a press invention suggested by the dubious evidence given by fruiterer Matthew Packer, as mentioned above.

On page 31 we cut to the upstairs room of the International Workers' Educational Club at 40 Berner Street, which overlooked Dutfield's Yard. The club was founded in 1884 by Jewish socialists. On the night in question there had been a meeting and a talk. This broke up around midnight, with various people staying behind for singing and discussion. The only real liberty that I have taken with this scene is the inclusion of William Morris. Morris often spoke or read his poetry at the club (see *JTR, The Uncensored Facts*), but I have no record of him having been there on the night in question. He is included both to mark his connection with the scene of the crime and to allow a

counterpoint between his poem "Love is Enough" and the brutal and loveless murder of Liz Stride taking place outside.

In the last panel of page 31 and in the first few panels of page 32 we see a passerby notice Liz Stride being flung to the ground and then being frightened off by Netley. This is a reconstruction of a woman in 1887 by a Jew named Lipski. This is all according to Paul Begg, who gives a much fuller and more detailed account of this fascinating incident than the necessarily brief and edited version depicted here. Begg's book is also the source for the depiction of the International Worker's Educational Club shown here, with its pictures of Marx on the wall.

Moving on to page 33, we see Gull finally contacted by the Masonic police constable dispatched earlier. Some incidental support for this is given in the testimony of Mrs. Fanny Mortimer of 36 Berner Street, who claimed that she heard the measured tread of a policeman pass her house at a time that Paul Begg indicates must have been approximate to 12:45 - 12:50, very close to the time of Stride's estimated death.

PAGE 34 - 40

This scene, which details the movements of Catherine Eddowes following her release from the drunk-tank at Bishopsgate Police station and culminating in her death in Mitre Square, is mostly culled from the information given in *JTR, The Uncensored Facts* and *The JTR A-Z*. This latter volume relates that Station Sergeant James Byfield heard Eddowes call out just after half-past twelve, asking when she could be released. His reply was as detailed here. At one o'clock, Eddowes was released, with the dialogue being pretty similar to that reported. She gave her name as Mary Ann Kelly, predicted that she would get a damn fine hiding when she got home and with a cheery "Goodnight, old cock" set off in the direction of Mitre Square at a little after one.

On page 36, in panel six, we see three gentlemen leaving a drinking establishment in the foreground while Netley and Catherine Eddowes are talking in the background. This corresponds to the testimony of Joseph Lawende, Joseph Hyam Levy and Harry Harris who, at roughly 1:35, saw Eddowes talking to a man in the covered entry of Church Passage, which led into Mitre Square. Within ten minutes she was dead, her injuries and mutilations corresponding to those that we see Gull inflict on pages 37, 38 and 39.

The strange Epiphany on page 40, during which Gull seems to see a vision of Mitre Square as it would look more than a century into his future, is entirely my own invention.

PAGE 41 - 46

The scene on these pages which intercuts between Gull writing his Masonic chalk-message in the doorway of Wentworth Model Buildings in Goulstone Street and the discovery of the bodies of his victims is compiled once more from *JTR*, *The Uncensored Facts* and *The JTR A-Z*. These books also confirm that Sir Charles Warren ordered that the message be scrubbed from the wall upon his arrival at the crime scene as depicted on page 46. The main bone of contention in this scene, as far as the literature on the subject is concerned, relates to whether the chalk message was in fact left by the murderer or was simply a piece of graffiti already on the wall when the murderer left the piece of bloodied apron there in the doorway. If the former is the case, then the dispute arises over whether the word "Juwes" should be seen as an indication of a Masonic hand behind the crimes.

Many commentators have claimed that Juwes, Stephen Knight to the contrary, is not a Masonic term at all. However, as mentioned earlier in these appendices, the book *Born in Blood* by John J. Robinson (Century Books, 1990) seems to confirm that "Juwes" is indeed a term of Masonic derivation, the authority of this identification strengthened by the fact that Robinson appears highly sympathetic to Freemasonry and had the help of Freemasons in compiling his book, with extensive access to their libraries. Of course, the fact that "Juwes" is a Masonic term does not necessarily mean that the author of the writing on the wall was a Freemason. He may well have been a simple illiterate, and his misspelling of "Jews" simply coincidental. As with much of the evidence surrounding these murders, the data is ambiguous; a shifting cloud of facts and factoids onto which we project the fictions that seem most appropriate to our times and our inclinations.

PAGES 47 & 48

These last two pages are an invention for story purposes. The scene is necessary in order to provide a rationale for Marie Kelly's increasing preoccupation with the Ripper murders in the weeks immediately prior to her death on the 9th of November, as testified to by Joseph Barnett and alluded to by most of the books relating to the murders that are mentioned above. Although it may seem to be stretching the facts a little to have Joseph Barnett already aware of the identity of the Berner Street victim before the Police themselves had positively identified her as Liz Stride, my own first-hand experience of murder in urban settings seems to suggest that "the word on the street" is often more accurate and more advanced than the information unearthed by the Police in the course of their investigations. One reason for this is the law of communication often quoted by Robert Anton Wilson which suggests that communication is only possible between equals: almost everybody living in the East End during the period in question would have had good reason to lie or withhold information when talking to the Police. Amongst themselves, of course, it would be a different story.

The delay in official identification of Elizabeth Stride is taken by A.P. Wolf, author of *Jack the Myth* (Robert Hale, 1993), as an indication that Stride was in fact murdered by her estranged boyfriend Michael Kidney, who turned up at the Police station next morning complaining about the inability of the Police to protect his ex-lover from the murderer. According to Wolf, this indicates that Kidney must have been the killer since even the Police at this point were unaware of the victim's identity. As stated above, however, I think it more likely that within a few hours of the crime a large part of the East End's population would have been aware of the broad facts concerning the murder by agency of a grapevine utterly unrelated to the one that was found or not found in Dutfield's Yard, clutched in Liz Stride's cold fingers.

Appendix to continue in future volumes of *From Hell*.